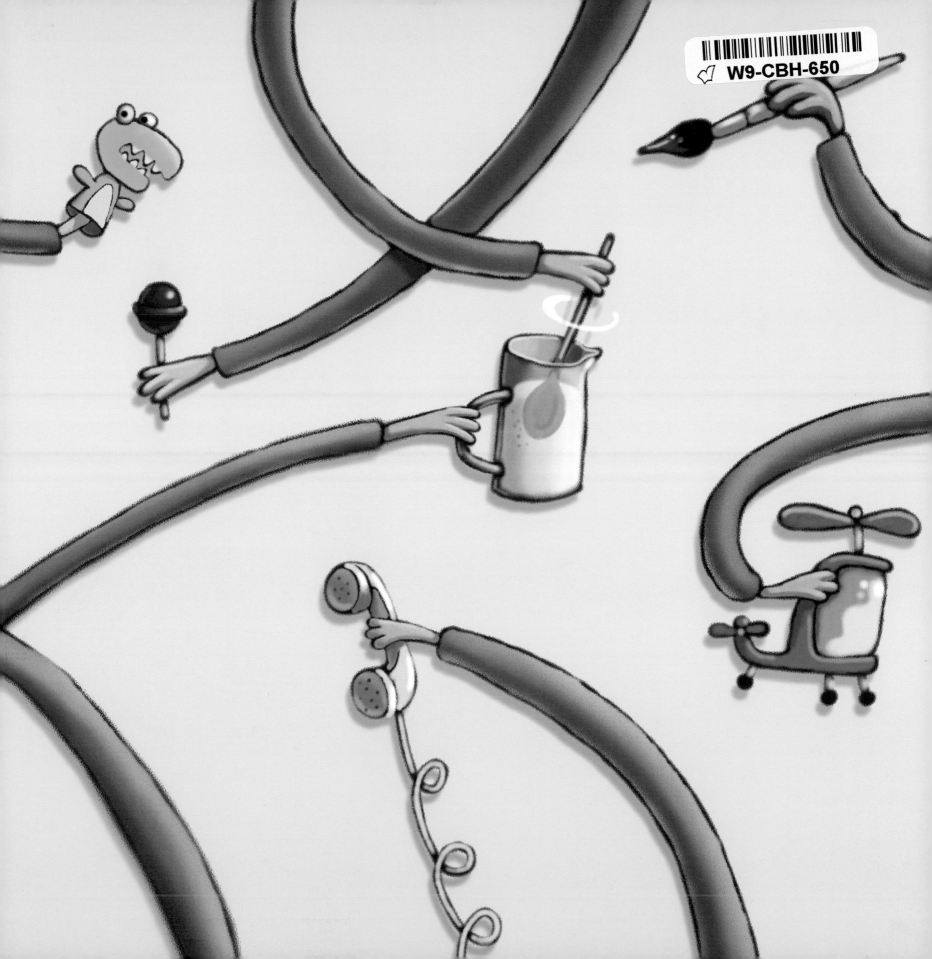

W9-CBH-650

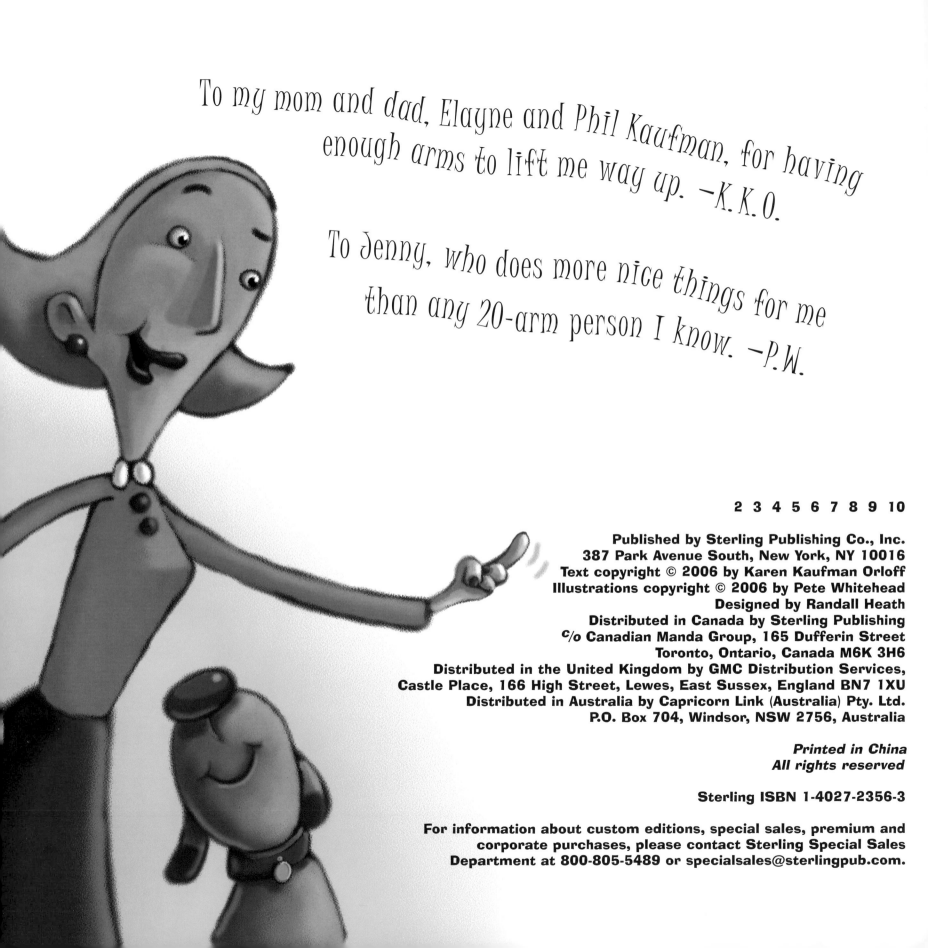

To my mom and dad, Elayne and Phil Kaufman, for having enough arms to lift me way up. —K.K.O.

To Jenny, who does more nice things for me than any 20-arm person I know. —P.W.

2 3 4 5 6 7 8 9 10

Published by Sterling Publishing Co., Inc.
387 Park Avenue South, New York, NY 10016
Text copyright © 2006 by Karen Kaufman Orloff
Illustrations copyright © 2006 by Pete Whitehead
Designed by Randall Heath
Distributed in Canada by Sterling Publishing
c/o Canadian Manda Group, 165 Dufferin Street
Toronto, Ontario, Canada M6K 3H6
Distributed in the United Kingdom by GMC Distribution Services,
Castle Place, 166 High Street, Lewes, East Sussex, England BN7 1XU
Distributed in Australia by Capricorn Link (Australia) Pty. Ltd.
P.O. Box 704, Windsor, NSW 2756, Australia

Printed in China
All rights reserved

Sterling ISBN 1-4027-2356-3

For information about custom editions, special sales, premium and
corporate purchases, please contact Sterling Special Sales
Department at 800-805-5489 or specialsales@sterlingpub.com.

If Mom Had Three Arms

By Karen Kaufman Orloff

Illustrated by
Pete Whitehead

Sterling Publishing Co., Inc.
New York

If Mom had three arms,
she could put on a show.

If Mom had five arms, she would look very smart.

If Mom had six arms, she could make some good art.

With seven arms, Mom would like playing pretend.

With eight arms, my mom
would be quick to make friends.

WHOOSH!

If Mom had nine arms, she would throw lots of pitches.

WHOOSH!

If Mom had ten arms, she could

Eleven arms? Wow! She'd be great at the griddle.

And if Mom had twelve arms, she'd be swell on the fiddle.

With thirteen arms, Mom could pour more lemonade.

If Mom had fifteen, she could keep the yard clean.

If Mom had sixteen, she could rule Halloween!

With seventeen arms, Mom could color the sky.

With eighteen long arms,
Mom could keep the town dry.

If Mom had nineteen, she could be the whole crew.

And with twenty arms,
she'd be president, too!

But Mom has two arms,
and that's perfectly fine,

'cause when my mom
hugs me . . .

I know they're both mine.